Seascape with Sharks and Dancer

A Play

by Don Nigro

SAMUEL FRENCH

FOUNDED 1830

New York Hollywood London Toronto

SAMUELFRENCH.COM

In the summer of 1984, *Seascape With Sharks and Dancer* was produced in the Black Swan Theatre at the Oregon Shakespearean Festival with the following cast:

TRACY ....Kamella Tate
BEN ....Paul Vincent O'Connor

It was directed by Dennis Bigelow. Scene Designer: William Bloodgood. Costume Designer: Jeannie Davidson. Lighting Designer: Robert Peterson. Music Composer: Todd Barton. Stage Manager: Kirk M. Boyd. Assistant Stage Manager: Edward D. O'Connell.

The play was first produced in May, 1974, in the Theatre Barn at the University of Massachusetts in Amherst, with Deborah Gibbs as Tracy and Thomas Keegan as Ben, directed by Marya Bednerik and Millie Tessler, stage managed by Amy Stark, with music by Thomas Keegan.

In March and April of 1980 Mark Cuddy directed a workshop production of the play at the Denver Center Theatre, with Jamie Newcomb as Ben and Kim Schwartz as Tracy. This production later moved to the Touchstone Theatre in Denver.

In February 1982 Gary Stewart directed the play at Indiana State University in Terre Haute, with Randy Noojin as Ben and Mindy Dyer as Tracy.

Those interested in using the excellent score for this play heard in the Oregon Shakespearean Festival production should contact the composer, Todd Barton, P.O. Box 763, Ashland, Oregon, 97520.

CHARACTERS

TRACY — about twenty
BEN — late twenties

Setting: A small decrepit beach house on Cape Cod.

There are two acts.

Seascape with Sharks
and Dancer

ACT ONE

Scene 1

Night. Ocean sounds. The living room of the beach house. Doors lead to a kitchen, a bedroom, and outside. TRACY is on the couch, wrapped in a blanket, her hair done up in a towel, eyes closed. She stretches and curls up like a cat; then, when she is perfectly still, she opens her eyes. She pulls the blanket tighter around herself and notices that she is alone. A moment of panic.

TRACY. Service. (*She listens.*) SERVICE! (*She finds a book and begins to pound on a table.*) SER-VICE! HEY! I WANT SOME SERVICE AROUND HERE! HEY! (*She pounds harder.*) HEYYYYYYYYYYYYYY!

BEN. (*sticking his head in from the kitchen door*) Do you have a problem?

TRACY. What lousy service. What kind of a rotten place are you running here, anyway?

BEN. A place where the guests aren't supposed to sit around screaming at the host. Banging Proust on the table is also frowned upon.

TRACY. Bullshit.

BEN. You want something?

TRACY. Yes. I want to know why you went off and left me.

BEN. I was making hot chocolate. I thought you were asleep.

5

TRACY. I don't drink in my sleep.

BEN. I wasn't making it for you.

TRACY. I don't think I like your attitude. I don't think I like your attitude at all.

BEN. I see you're feeling better.

TRACY. Better than what?

BEN. Than when I fished you out. You want some hot chocolate?

TRACY. No. Yes.

BEN. (*turning to go*) Okay.

TRACY. Where you going?

BEN. In the kitchen to get the hot chocolate. Is that all right with you?

TRACY. Oh. Sure. (*He hesitates.*) Well go on. What are you looking at?

BEN. I'm not sure yet. (*He goes into the kitchen. From there:*) Do you have a name?

TRACY. Yes. (*pause*)

BEN. Why don't you tell me what it is?

TRACY. What do I look like my name is?

BEN. Desdemona?

TRACY. No.

BEN. Esmerelda?

TRACY. No.

BEN. (*entering with two cups of hot chocolate*) Sacajawea?

TRACY. Don't spill it. You're going to spill it.

BEN. I'm not going to spill it.

TRACY. What's YOUR name, smart ass?

BEN. What name do you like?

TRACY. You look like a Charles.

BEN. (*giving her one cup*) I don't feel like a Charles. Watch out, it's hot.

TRACY. (*accepting it rather cautiously*) Yes you do. Ouch. It's hot.

BEN. How does a Charles feel?

TRACY. Like a jerk. (*blowing on the hot chocolate*) Hey, it's even got mushrunes in it.

BEN. (*sitting on the other end of the couch*) MushROOMS.

TRACY. That's what I said. Anyway, they're marsh-mallows, stupid, not mushrunes. Don't sit so close. What are you smiling at?

BEN. Nothing.

TRACY. Only crazy people smile at nothing. I'm not going to sit here and drink chocolate and mushrunes with some character that drags me out of the water so he can laugh at me.

BEN. You want me to throw you back in?

TRACY. I don't allow people to laugh at me. I just won't have it.

BEN. Sorry. I promise not to laugh.

TRACY. Well you'd better not. (*They sip in silence for a moment, watching each other, suspicious, TRACY rather like a wild animal.*) You're smiling. You smiled. What the HELL is so funny? Are you thinking about me naked? I bet that's what it is. You think you're one up on me because you saw me naked. Well I don't care. Why should I care? Am I ashamed of my body?

BEN. I hope not.

TRACY. Right. I bet you wonder what I was doing out there in the ocean in the middle of the night, don't you?

BEN. Looked like you were drowning.

TRACY. HAH. What a small mind. Guess.

BEN. I don't want to guess.

TRACY. Go on, guess. I want you to guess.

BEN. Were you scuba diving?
TRACY. No.
BEN. Tuna fishing?
TRACY. Wrong wrong wrong.
BEN. I give up.
TRACY. You give up too easy. I bet you give up all the time. I bet you give up at least once every three or four hours. Every twenty minutes, maybe. I can tell things like that. I'm very perceptive about people. I bet you're a very ineffectual person.
BEN. You can tell that from just looking at me?
TRACY. Not just that. There are lots of clues. You can see a lot if you observe.
BEN. Like what?
TRACY. Like you just said twice you gave up. Like the way you drink your hot chocolate, like you're protecting it from something. Like the way you apologized for laughing at me.
BEN. I shouldn't have apologized?
TRACY. Of course you should have. But you didn't have to. But you did.
BEN. And that proves I'm ineffectual?
TRACY. Either that or just dumb.
BEN. My GOODNESS you're perceptive.
TRACY. Thank you.
BEN. Anything else you'd like to reveal to me about my true self?
TRACY. (*sipping chocolate, thinking about it*) You're also — uh — chicken.
BEN. I'm a chicken?
TRACY. You're afraid of things.
BEN. What things?
TRACY. Things. Everything. You're afraid of me. Probably the dark. Cockroaches.

BEN. What gave me away?

TRACY. The way your face moved when I told you you were ineffectual. And the way you sit there and look at me like I was somebody. If you weren't afraid of me you wouldn't have to pay attention, would you?

BEN. Does that make sense?

TRACY. I can tell chicken when I smell it.

BEN. You're sort of a chicken expert.

TRACY. I've had a lot of experience. With chickens.

BEN. People? Or poultry?

TRACY. Exactly. I used to wake up and hear chickens all the time.

BEN. You lived on a farm.

TRACY. No, in New York City. I may have heard the only surviving group of wild chickens in all of New York City.

BEN. Where did these chickens come from?

TRACY. From eggs.

BEN. No, I mean—

TRACY. I'd wake up in the middle of the night and I'd be hearing these chickens, see, and I'd wake up the guy I lived with—he was just some guy I lived with—

BEN. And you'd wake him up.

TRACY. And he'd tell me there weren't any chickens, go back to sleep, Christ—he called me Christ—Christ, what a bimbo, he'd say—he was a humorist, he had a dry sense of humor, like an old soda cracker—but he was wrong. There WERE SO chickens. And I kept hearing them.

BEN. You're an exceptional person.

TRACY. I know it. I was dancing. In the sea. That's what I was doing. Dancing.

BEN. You were dancing?

TRACY. Yes.

BEN. In the ocean.

TRACY. Yes.

BEN. You weren't drowning a little, too?

TRACY. Positively not.

BEN. You coughed up an awful lot of water.

TRACY. I was thirsty. Hey, this is really a dump you've got here, you know that?

BEN. Well thank you.

TRACY. I mean, I guess it's all right if this is what you like. I guess. (*She gets up and walks around, looking the place over, picking up things to examine, not putting them back in the same places. She has a little trouble getting around gracefully with the blanket around her.*) Different kinds of people like different kinds of things, I guess. It isn't so bad.

BEN. For a dump.

TRACY. Yeah.

BEN. Do you want some more hot chocolate?

TRACY. Yes. No.

BEN. Are you sure?

TRACY. I said no.

BEN. Would you like something to eat?

TRACY. Don't be an obsequious host.

BEN. Sorry.

TRACY. And don't be sorry.

BEN. All right.

TRACY. And don't always agree with me.

BEN. You're kind of hard to please, aren't you?

TRACY. And don't contradict me.

BEN. I didn't contradict you.

TRACY. See? (*He gives up and sits there in silence.*) I was dancing.

BEN. All right, you were dancing.

TRACY. Do you have a telephone?

BEN. No.

TRACY. Good.

BEN. Why is it good?

TRACY. Because I don't want any phone calls.

BEN. How could anybody know you're here?

TRACY. How do YOU know if anybody knows I'm here? Do you live here all by yourself?

BEN. Yes.

TRACY. That figures.

BEN. What figures?

TRACY. You seem to be sort of a eunuch type.

BEN. Now wait a minute—

TRACY. It's all right. I don't guess you can help it.

BEN. Just what are you trying to prove, anyway?

TRACY. I'm not trying to prove anything. Why should I be trying to prove anything?

BEN. I've known you about forty-five minutes and already you're telling me I'm a chicken and a eunuch.

TRACY. And ineffectual.

BEN. That sounds to me like you're trying to prove something.

TRACY. Like what?

BEN. I don't know. If you're trying to prove you're cute, you're not succeeding. Obnoxious, you've achieved.

TRACY. Well, drop dead.

BEN. I mean, didn't I just drag you out of the ocean when you were drowning?

TRACY. Dancing. I WAS DANCING.

BEN. Didn't I pump you out and dry you off—

TRACY. I WAS DANCING.

BEN. —and give you hot chocolate and mushmellows—

TRACY. Marshmellons.

BEN. Isn't this MY house and isn't that MY blanket and didn't I just—

TRACY. Why are you screaming these stupid rhetorical questions at four o'clock in the morning? And why are you getting so mad at me?

BEN. WHO'S MAD? AM I MAD? I'M NOT MAD. SHIT, I'M ON TOP OF THE WORLD.

TRACY. Proves my point. Insecurity. And besides, if you're not a eunus—

BEN. Eunuch.

TRACY. —then how come you didn't rape me? You had me all naked and wet and helpless and everything and all you did was give me hot chocolate.

BEN. I'm a eunuch because I didn't rape you?

TRACY. No, you didn't rape me because you're a eunuch. So there. (*She sticks out her tongue.*)

BEN. All right. I'll rape you. (*He lunges at her.*)

TRACY. (*getting away, horrified*) Get your goddamn paws off me, Lucius.

BEN. Oh, so you don't want me to rape you.

TRACY. Of course I don't want you to rape me.

BEN. All right then, that makes you a lady eunuch.

TRACY. That's dumb. God that's dumb. There's no such thing as a lady eunuch. Boy, are you stupid.

BEN. Actually, I didn't rape you because you're homely.

TRACY. (*shocked*) I am not homely. You're homely. And stupid and chicken and, and rude, and ungrate-ful—

BEN. I'M ungrateful?

TRACY. You stink. Just where do you think you get off talking to me like that, anyway? I didn't ask you to drag me into your stupid dump, did I?

BEN. Okay, take it easy, I'm—

TRACY. Easy your uncle Fred's ass. I'm not homely and I never was homely and I'm not ever going to be homely. (*She is throwing things at him and knocking over furniture.*) I'm beautiful and people love me and you're jealous because you're ugly and nobody loves you and you want to die.

BEN. (*trying to get a hold on her*) Wait a minute. Hey.

TRACY. (*struggling*) Okay, buster, you just better let me go. You pig. Don't you try and rape me, you eunuch. (*She manages to get an elbow in his groin.*)

BEN. OWWWWWWWWWWWWWWWW.

TRACY. Serves you right. And you can just take your clunky house and your stupid mushrunes and your moldy old towel—(*She wrenches the towel from her hair and throws it at him. Her hair is long and still a bit wet.*)—and your precious old blanket which for your information has got lice in it—(*She is stomping towards the door and trying to take the blanket off, but it is wrapped around her in such a way that she gets tangled in it, steps on one end and lands on the floor.*) I'm getting out of here.

BEN. Wait a minute. (*He makes his way painfully over to her and tries to help her up.*)

TRACY. (*trying desperately to get up, hair in her face, getting more and more tangled in the blanket*) I HATE THIS I HATE THIS I HATE THIS I HATE THIS. (*She begins swinging her arms wildly at him.*)

BEN. (*trying to help her up and protect his groin*) You can't go out there with nothing on.

TRACY. (*still swinging and struggling*) Naked came I into this dump—WATCH IT—(*increasing frustration*)—and naked shall I return unto the fucking sea from whence I fucking came. Get your slimey hands off me, you pervert. (*She connects a rather violent blow in the middle of his face. He falls over backwards.*) What's the matter, SISSY? No more fight left in you?

BEN. (*holding one palm up to his face*) My nose is bleeding.

TRACY. (*gratified*) Oh, for corn sake, what a baby.

BEN. Christ, with a punch like that you could bleed Jack Dempsey.

TRACY. I don't want to hear about your stupid friends. You're not bleeding.

BEN. (*holding out bloody fingers*) What's this? Fingerpaint?

TRACY. Son of a gun. How about that. You ARE bleeding.

BEN. (*getting up, with ruffled dignity, still holding his nose*) Isn't that amazing? What a piece of work is man. Strike him violently in the middle of his face and, like magic, red glop comes pouring out. (*He moves rather shakily over to lie on the couch. TRACY watches guiltily.*) Well? Aren't you going to take the damn blanket off and go running through town naked? Maybe we can get you a horse. How about a bugle?

TRACY. (*trying to sound tough, but clearly upset*) Don't stick your fingers in your nose. God what a jerk. (*She moves around nervously, her hands pulling her hair from her eyes, glancing briefly towards the door, then back to him.*)

BEN. What are you waiting for? A streetcar?

TRACY. Is it stopping?

BEN. No, it's not stopping. You want to come over and punch me again to make sure?

TRACY. (*deciding, against her better judgement*) Oh, well, all right, shit. (*She tightens the blanket around her and storms in his direction. He cringes, but she moves past him and goes into the kitchen. Loud banging and clanking noises.*)

BEN. What are you doing in there? Stealing silver-ware?

TRACY. Shut up and get your fingers out of your nose.

BEN. I'll stick my fingers anywhere I want to.

TRACY. Fat chance.

BEN. What?

TRACY. You're just going to make it bleed more. Where do you keep your ice?

BEN. In the cookie jar. Where do you think I keep my ice?

TRACY. (*Returning with one dishtowel wrapped around ice, another damp one, and some paper towels. She sits on the couch with him, all business.*) All right. Raise your head. (*She picks up his head by the hair.*)

BEN. OWW.

TRACY. Shut up. (*She puts the compress under his neck, then drops his head into her lap. Then she tears strips of paper towel, wads them up, and begins to stuff them into his nostrils.*) Hold still.

BEN. What are you doing? What are you sticking up my nose? I'll suffocate.

TRACY. Breathe through your mouth, stupid.

BEN. What's that supposed to—

TRACY. LOOK, JUST SHUT THE FUCK UP, ALL RIGHT? (*He does. She wipes the blood from his face with a damp dishtowel.*) Now just sit still for a minute and don't talk. God, what a dork. (*She puts the dishtowel on his forehead.*) There. Isn't that nice? Aren't I a nice little Nurse Jane Fuzzy Wuzzy? Do you have a comb, Bozo?

BEN. You want to stick that up my nose, too?

TRACY. I might. Shut up. (*He reaches into his back pocket and finds a comb, which she takes with one finger and a thumb.*) Eccch. It's got crud all over it. (*She wipes it on his shirt.*) I guess it'll have to do. (*She begins combing out her hair.*) Bleccch. What a mess. Ouch. Tangles. Ouch. Have you got a brush or something?

BEN. I have a dog brush. How about a paint brush? Sagebr—

TRACY. (*matter of factly*) Shut up. (*He shuts up.*) That's a good boy. You mind very well.

BEN. And I'm housebroken. (*She gives him a dirty warning look and he looks contrite, shuts up, puts his finger to his lips.*)

TRACY. (*continuing to comb*) You understand I'm just sticking around for a minute or two to make sure you don't fingerpaint yourself to death. Then I'm leaving right away. So don't get any funny ideas. (*pause*) I only hit you because you asked for it. You should be more careful where you're sticking your face and things. You should learn self defense. And don't call people homely. That's not high class behavior, Jack. (*They look at each other; pause.*)

BEN. This feels good. I like this. (*Pause; they look at each other. TRACY gets up abruptly, and his head clunks loudly on the couch.*)

TRACY. You ought to take better care of this place. It's a mess. (*She begins to straighten up the mess she's made.*) It wouldn't look half so bad if you'd just take a little trouble to keep it cleaned up. Cleanliness is next to tenderness.

BEN. Godliness.

TRACY. That too. You're not supposed to talk. It'll bleed more.

BEN. Can I talk if I don't move my nose?

TRACY. I don't think you CAN talk without moving your nose. (*coming over to look*) Let me see. Say something.

BEN. What should I say?

TRACY. I don't care. Tell me a story.

BEN. I don't know any stories.

TRACY. (*sitting down beside him*) Tell me a fucking story. I love stories. Stories are my bread and butter. And if your nose moves once, you have to shut up. Okay?

BEN. I don't have any stories.

TRACY. Nobody's as dumb as that. You just don't want to. Forget it. (*She starts to get up. He pulls her back down.*)

BEN. I'll try.

TRACY. You don't really want to.

BEN. I want to. I want to.

TRACY. Okay.

BEN. Uh, well, lets see, once upon a time —

TRACY. Your nose is moving.

BEN. No it's not.

TRACY. It certainly is too. I saw it. It moved. You lose.

BEN. What do you mean, I lose? If I can't talk then you don't get a story.

TRACY. Oh. Well, in that case, I'm leaving. (*She starts up again. He pulls her down by the blanket.*)

BEN. Wait a minute. Why don't you tell ME a story. Show me how it's done.

TRACY. I don't think I want to.

BEN. Chicken.

TRACY. I'm not chicken. I just don't know which story to tell.

BEN. Buck-buck-bu-GAWK. Bu-GAWK.

TRACY. What do you want? Hansel and Gretel? The Story of O?

BEN. Tell me a true life adventure. I love true life adventures.

TRACY. I don't feel like it.

BEN. I'll talk. I'll sing opera and bleed to death all over your foot.

TRACY. Oh, awright, awright, smart ass. Here it comes. Story. You ready?

BEN. I'm ready.

TRACY. If I'm going to tell this story, you've got to shut your mouth and keep your nose in place, okay?

BEN. Okay.

TRACY. Christ. Well, once upon a time there was a little girl. And she was a very bright little girl, and rather wicked, and she wandered all over the country hitching rides and shacking up until she'd been just about everything and done almost everywhere, although she was in fact only twenty and a half years old. Am I going too fast for you?

BEN. I think I can handle it.

TRACY. Shut up. Now you wouldn't have thought she could survive very long this way, since she wasn't very big and she didn't look very strong but she was pretty tough all the same, and so finally this little girl found herself plunk in the middle of New York City, all shacked up nicely with a handsome prince who also pushed a little dope on the side because there wasn't much money in the handsome prince racket if you were shacked up with some drippy-nosed girl, and she had a job in this sick department store selling orthopedic brassieres and one day her little squidlike manager squirted over the carpet towards her and said she was fired for setting a bad example by not wearing this incredible bra-thing she was supposed to be selling to these saggy baggy old ladies, so she went home to her nice little cave feeling sad but also happy because she'd have this funny story to tell the handsome prince and part time pusher about the little squiddy manager, and she opened the door and the cave was absolutely empty. The handsome prince had taken everything except the cockroaches and skipped away to Miami without so much as a goodbye tumble on the daybed. She really didn't care much because the prince had a pronounced inability to hear chickens and several other faults which I forget, but she had a little scream-ing fit, just because she felt like it, and then she got up off the floor and took her last subway token out of her pocket and said goodbye to the cockroaches and went to Coney Island and snuck into the aquarium there and saw all the fishes and crap and this wounded octopus and some big dumb white baby whales but she wasn't paying really any special attention until she got to the shark tank. She was standing in front of the shark tank and looking at these stupid sharks, see, and she began to be really fascinated by these sharks. Their eyes were wide open and they never blinked or anything and they were staring through the glass about four inches from you and they had big rows of ugly horrible teeth and they came right up to your nose and looked at you and didn't see you and knew you were there all the same. And these sharks would swim by and look at her with the eyes staring and the rows of saw teeth and everything and they were so very stupid looking that the girl just stood there and looked at the sharks that were stupid and staring with big empty eyes and rows and rows of teeth gliding in the cold water back and forth and back and teeth and eyes and vacant stares like maniacs and they were waiting for her. (*Pause; she sits there for a moment quietly, seeing sharks.*)

BEN. (*not touching her*) Hey—

TRACY. Don't touch me.

BEN. (*quiet*) Listen, uh—

TRACY. (*snapping out of it with a bit too much enthusiasm*) I've never really been abducted like this.

BEN. Abducted?

TRACY. Yes. You abducted me. Isn't that a federal offense?

BEN. You haven't been—

TRACY. I have too. I have been abducted. Not inducted or deducted. Not interducted or subducted or motherducted or Donaldducted but AB-ducted. ABDUCTED. I HAVE BEEN ABDUCTED.

BEN. All right, you've been abducted. Congratulations.

TRACY. (*modestly*) Thank you.

BEN. (*using thumb as microphone*) Tell me, miss, what does it feel like to be abducted?

TRACY. (*her face for a moment quite close to his*) It's REALLY boring. (*She bites his thumb.*)

BEN. OWWWW.

TRACY. (*getting up and moving away*) Are you done bleeding, or what?

BEN. Sure. Yes. Can I take these things out of my nose?

TRACY. No, wait a little bit. When I pull them out you'll take a nice deep breath through your nose and this enormous clot of blood will drop down into your throat and you'll swallow it with a big gulp and it'll be like swallowing a mashed up toad.

BEN. Great imagination you've got there, kid.

TRACY. I'm very imaginative. Creative. I'm very intelligent. You can see that, can't you?

BEN. Oh, yes.

TRACY. Don't patronize me.

BEN. I wasn't —

TRACY. You just said that to make me happy.

BEN. How could I possibly know what would make you happy?

TRACY. By paying attention. At least people that don't like you pay attention to you sometimes. People that like you never do.

BEN. Which kind am I?

TRACY. You're just a creep with a bloody nose. Who cares? Don't you have anything around here to eat? I'm starving. Do all you abductors starve your abductees? Why don't you go into the kitchen and make me a ham sandwich. With cheese and mustard and some sweet pickle.

BEN. How do you know I have all that?

TRACY. I peeked. Come on. I fixed your nose, didn't I? It's the least you can do.

BEN. Okay. Why not. You want swiss or cream cheese?

TRACY. Both. And don't put the cheese together. Put the cream cheese on one side of the ham and the swiss cheese on the other.

BEN. (*getting up and going into the kitchen*) Yes ma'am.

TRACY. And the pickle on the cream cheese side. And salt and pepper on the swiss cheese side. And mustard on that side, too. The swiss cheese side.

BEN. You seem to know what you want.

TRACY. I know exactly what I want. At all times and in all situations. That's my trademark. Have you got potato chips?

BEN. (*from the kitchen*) Yes.

TRACY. Well, I don't want any.

BEN. All right.

TRACY. No, give me some.

BEN. All right.

TRACY. I think I'd rather have pretzels.

BEN. I don't have any pretzels.

TRACY. That's what I want.

BEN. You'll take potato chips and like it.

TRACY. Hurry up.

BEN. Why don't you come in here and help me?

TRACY. (*exploring*) I'm the guest.

BEN. Oh.

TRACY. Hurry up, all right?

BEN. Just a minute.

TRACY. Do you want to hear the rest of my story?

BEN. There's more?

TRACY. (*examining the contents of drawers*) Yes, there's more.

BEN. Okay. Go ahead.

TRACY. (*She has found a ring.*) Why should I?

BEN. I don't know. It was a thrilling story.

TRACY. (*admiring the ring, trying it on*) It was an awful story.

BEN. Then don't tell any more of it.

TRACY. (*slipping the ring off her finger and hiding it in the folds of the blanket*) So after she got done looking at the sharks she went out onto the beach there at Coney Island only it was about five in the afternoon and nobody was there, it was all empty, just her and the sand and the trash and the dirty water and some sea gulls. And she wondered if all oceans were as dirty and as dead as that, or whether the Pacific Ocean was maybe cleaner than the Atlantic Ocean because it hadn't been used as much or something, so she stole a few things from the department store where she used to work and hocked them and got on the Greyhound to Pittsburgh, where a woman in a funny hat stole her ticket but some old Greek guy in the coffee shop was driving to Woonsocket Rhode Island so she thought what the hell and from there she got a ride up to Provincetown with some acid freaks in a purple Volkswagen and on the way she got out to look at the water and they forgot her or something and drove off and she hung around there until it was night and then she started to smell sharks. The end.

BEN. This girl steals things, does she?

TRACY. (*startled and a bit guilty*) Just in the story. (*She takes the ring out and looks at it.*) Just when she has to. (*In a rather bad humor she puts the ring back in the drawer where she found it.*) And only from rich people.

BEN. Like Robin Hood.

TRACY. Don't get sarcastic. You ever been poor?

BEN. (*entering with a tray on which are two sandwiches, two more cups of hot chocolate, and a bowl of potato chips*) Not down to my last bus token. I guess I shouldn't criticize this girl in the story if I've never been down to my last bus token.

TRACY. (*starting to eat immediately*) Damn right.

BEN. I've never been rich.

TRACY. Now you tell ME a story.

BEN. I don't have any stories.

TRACY. Bullshit.

BEN. Don't eat so fast. You'll choke to death.

TRACY. (*with full mouth*) BULLSHIT.

BEN. On second thought go ahead.

TRACY. You SAID. You said if I showed you how, you would. You promised and anybody who promises and then chickens out is a no good dirty—

BEN. What kind of story do you want?

TRACY. (*eating the sandwich voraciously and periodically grabbing bunches of potato chips to stuff into her mouth*) That's YOUR problem. I mean, anybody who's too dumb to even—

BEN. Once upon a time, uh, once upon a time there was a bewildered young man.

TRACY. What bewildered him?

BEN. He was born that way. It was a congenital defect.

TRACY. Uh huh. Hold it. (*She reaches over and pulls the towels out of his nostrils with a jerk.*) Okay. Go on. (*BEN swallows a great gulp and looks a bit sick.*) Why aren't you eating your sandwich?

BEN. I'm not hungry.

TRACY. Well talk then.

BEN. Uh, so this young man was walking along the beach one night.

TRACY. Around here?

BEN. Pretty close.

TRACY. How come?

BEN. How come what?

TRACY. How come was he walking at night on the beach?

BEN. (*irritated at the constant interruptions*) I don't know. Why not? He's despondent, his goldfish died, how should I know?

TRACY. I was just asking. You don't have to bite my head off.

BEN. And he spotted this thing floating in the ocean.

TRACY. A bottle with a note in it.

BEN. No.

TRACY. A corpse? A treasure chest?

BEN. It was a wounded bird.

TRACY. What kind of stupid story is that?

BEN. Will you shut up?

TRACY. Okay, okay. You want that other sandwich?

BEN. I don't think so.

TRACY. Good. (*She grabs his sandwich and takes a bite out of it.*)

BEN. You haven't finished yours yet.

TRACY. Don't worry about it. You just go on with your dumb story. What kind of bird was it?

BEN. A loon. A wounded featherless loon. A looney bird.

TRACY. And how did it get wounded?

BEN. Sharks. (*pause*)

TRACY. I think this is the dumbest story I ever heard.

BEN. Good. I'll stop.

TRACY. No, go ahead, what the hell.

BEN. So, he pulled this bird out of the water, see, and the loon began to shriek at him. And it shrieked and shrieked and shrieked.

TRACY. What did it do that for?

BEN. Only God knows for sure, but possibly, in its own peculiar native looney bird language, the bird was asking for help.

TRACY. Do you mind if I puke on your foot?

BEN. Do I have a choice?

TRACY. That is the most revolting story I ever heard in my life. That's disgusting. What kind of self-respecting looney bird goes around shrieking its head off for help to some perfect stranger who happens also to be a royal asshole?

BEN. You wanted a story. That's the best I can do.

TRACY. Well, it's awful. Hey, what do you do? I mean, besides sitting around making hot chocolate and bleeding a lot, what do you actually DO?

BEN. I'm a writer.

TRACY. Yes, but, I mean, really, what do you DO?

BEN. I'm a writer.

TRACY. YOU'RE a WRITER? (*She giggles a lot. She controls herself. She starts all over again.*) My GOD. What do you write? Gum wrappers? Cornflakes boxes?

BEN. I'm writing a novel.

TRACY. But you aren't actually living off that, right?

BEN. I work in a library.

TRACY. That sounds more like it. (*She looks at him and discovers that this time she has hurt his feelings rather more substantially than before.*) How's your nose?

BEN. It's all right. (*long pause*)

TRACY. (*uncomfortable*) I bet you're not such a bad writer. I bet a lot of writers start out working in libraries. I mean, it isn't anything to be ashamed of, or anything. (*She sees that this has made it worse, and there is suddenly something like despair in her voice.*) Are you going to be mad at me now? (*She sniffs.*)

BEN. (*looking at her, surprised by her tone*) Uh, well, no, I don't think so. (*Pause. They exchange a brief look. BEN smiles. TRACY smiles back, insecure, gets nervous, tries to occupy herself with her hair. She combs.*)

TRACY. That nose of yours has marvelous recuperative powers. You ought to put that in the circus. (*She sniffs again, a rather long slurp. Another tangle.*) God, what a mess. (*pause*) My hair. (*pause*) Is a mess.

BEN. It looks nice.

TRACY. It's a straggley mess. (*She is shivering. She sniffs again.*)

BEN. You're catching cold.

TRACY. Am not. (*snnnnnnnnnnniffffff*)

BEN. You've got the shivers and your nose is running. Maybe you should go to bed.

TRACY. I knew that was coming.

BEN. (*starting to help her up*) Come on.

TRACY. (*violently*) Don't you TOUCH me. CREEP. WRITER.

BEN. I'm not going to do anything to you.

TRACY. You're damn right you're not.

BEN. God. Little Miss Virginal Virtue, who comes in from running around in the altogether in the middle of the night and is horrified when I touch her royal sacred elbow.

TRACY. Don't play innocent with me. I know you. I know what you are. Gold plated shit on a stick. It's all deals. You treat me nice and I let you touch my elbow. You say nice things to me and I let you kiss me. You take me to the zoo and I let you feel me up. You buy me a Whitman Sampler and I let you crawl all over me in the back seat. Etcetera. Well, I'm sick of that. I hate you. I've never hated anybody so much in my whole life. (*She sneezes quite dramatically.*)

BEN. I'm sorry I don't come up to your standards.

TRACY. I BET you are. (*sneeze*) Shit. I'm leaving. (*She makes several attempts to get up, but the tangled blanket and the sagging couch are too much for her. She ends up just sitting there.*) Oh, fuck.

BEN. You're tired, and you're catching cold, and I just wanted to help you, God knows why, all right?

TRACY. Liar. Ulterior motives. Don't bother me. (*She puts her head down on one arm, raises it to sniff loudly, then puts it down again.*) Traitor. Shark lover. (*sniff*)

BEN. (*getting a box of tissues and plunking it down in front of her*) Here. Blow your nose. (*He gets some other blankets and a pillow; she yanks out a tissue.*)

You can stay here on the couch. (*She blows her nose loudly. He puts the pillow at one end of the couch and wraps another blanket around her, over the twisted one.*) Lean back. Come on. You can't even sit up, you're so tired.

TRACY. I can sit up if I want to. (*But she allows him to lean her back until her head is resting on the pillow.*) I just don't want to. (*afterthought*) You drip. (*He tucks the blanket around her.*)

BEN. You didn't finish either one of your sandwiches.

TRACY. I never finish anything. You never lose anything if you don't finish it. Take my advice. Don't finish your novel. You'll lose it.

BEN. Are you going to be all right here?

TRACY. You sure you're not going to sneak out here and rape me in the middle of the night?

BEN. Pretty sure.

TRACY. (*sniff*) You're pretty weird, you know that?

BEN. Am I?

TRACY. People who aren't going to rape me usually throw me out after the first twenty minutes. They think I'm crazy.

BEN. Why would they think that?

TRACY. Beats ME. (*Sniffffff*)

BEN. Can you get some rest now?

TRACY. I guess. (*He turns off the light. She panics.*) HEY. Don't do that. Haven't you got a night light or something?

BEN. (*turning on a small light*) That all right?

TRACY. Sure.

BEN. I'm going in to bed. Good night.

TRACY. You're going in to bed?

BEN. Yes.

TRACY. Right now?

BEN. Do you want something?

TRACY. No.

BEN. Do you want me to stay and sit with you?

TRACY. No.

BEN. Are you sure?

TRACY. Of course I'm sure.

BEN. Well, good night, then.

TRACY. (*stopping him with her voice*) You like me, don't you?

BEN. Maybe.

TRACY. It isn't my fault.

BEN. I know.

TRACY. You better not like me.

BEN. Why not?

TRACY. (*sniff*) I'm going to get up in the morning and walk right out of here. (*sniff*) I bet you think I'm afraid to be alone out here. (*sniff*) Go to bed. Get lost.

BEN. All right.

TRACY. (*stopping him again with her voice*) I think you must be crazy to let some strange person into your house like this. I could be some kind of psychopathic ax murderer or some weirdo opium freak or a Martian vampire or something, for all you know, out here in the dark.

BEN. Would you like—

TRACY. I mean, let's face it, the world's all sharks, right? What are you just standing there for? What do you think you're looking at? (*brief pause*) If you touch me I'll scream.

BEN. I'm going to bed. If you need anything I'll be right in here. (*Pause; he looks at her.*) Nobody here is going to use you or hurt you or make you do anything you don't want to do, or be anybody you don't want to be. You understand that?

TRACY. Yes.

BEN. Do you believe it?

TRACY. No. (*He looks at her for a moment, then turns and goes into the bedroom. She sits there, nervous and unhappy, her hands moving over the blanket, smoothing her hair, messing it up again. She pulls the blanket up around her to just under her eyes and looks around the room with growing suspicion. She gets up and starts moving about the room, tugging at the blanket as she goes, straightening things and then messing them up again, always just a little unsure about what is directly behind her. Finally she goes to the door of the bedroom, hesitates, sighs, tucks the blanket around her once more, crosses herself, and goes in.*)

BEN. (*from the bedroom*) You forgot the light. (*TRACY stomps back out, fumes, then turns off the light and stomps back in, slamming the door behind her.*)

SCENE 2

Late the next morning; voices from the bedroom.

TRACY. I did not either.

BEN. You did so too.

TRACY. (*entering, wearing the tops of a pair of men's pyjamas*) I do not have nightmares either. (*She heads for the box of tissues by the couch and blows her nose loudly.*)

BEN. (*entering, wearing the bottoms of the pyjamas*) You had one last night. You were yelling and crying and all twisted up.

TRACY. I don't remember that. What were you doing while I was all twisted up?

BEN. I got a hold of you and untwisted you some and then we—

TRACY. THAT part I remember. (*blowing her nose again and looking over the room*) Boy, what a slob you are. How can you stand to live amidst all this filth?

BEN. It's not filth. It's the mess you made last night.

TRACY. (*beginning to clean things up, returning for tissues periodically*) Did you ever sleep before with a girl with a terminal head cold?

BEN. I don't think so.

TRACY. I guess my nose must have dripped all over your mouth and your neck and your ears and everything.

BEN. I didn't notice. What was your nightmare about?

TRACY. I don't know. What does anybody dream about? What do YOU dream about?

BEN. Old houses, mostly.

TRACY. That's pretty weird.

BEN. I know. I just keep walking through these old houses and down stairways and through passages and into other dark old houses.

TRACY. And that's it? That's all that happens?

BEN. Pretty much.

TRACY. Aren't there people in it?

BEN. No.

TRACY. You must be sick. You should see a doctor. Nobody has dreams without people in them. It must mean something.

BEN. Maybe it means I don't know anybody.

TRACY. What would you do if you were having this

dream and you're in this old dark house or whatever and you turn this corner and pull back this curtain or open the closet or something and there all of a sudden is a real live actual flesh and blood human person right there? What would you do?

BEN. (*grasping the back of her pyjamas as she goes by and pulling her onto his lap*) I'd grab her.

TRACY. But what if she was repulsive or obnoxious or something?

BEN. Obnoxious is in the eye of the beholder. (*It looks like a kiss is coming up, but at the last moment she disengages.*)

TRACY. I think I'd better be going.

BEN. Going where?

TRACY. I don't know. Kansas City. Luxembourg. The Yukon. Someplace.

BEN. You mean go AWAY. Permanent.

TRACY. Yeah. Permanent. (*Pause; he looks at her.*) Why not? What's there to do around here?

BEN. How you going to get to Luxembourg?

TRACY. Maybe I'll go home first and bum some money from my father and then go to Luxembourg. I bet you thought I didn't have any family or anything. I bet you thought that. I have a father—retch, vomit, gag—and a mother, who's not so bad when she keeps her mouth shut, and I have a whole bunch of brothers and sisters, too, and I'm the only one that doesn't have acne. Honest. Clean living is the answer. I was supposed to be going to see them, only we don't get along.

BEN. Why not?

TRACY. I don't know. My father wants me to start going to college again and get a job and all. I'm just not what they wanted.

BEN. What did they want?

TRACY. Miss America. Lots of teeth and vacant eyes and big boobs. Straight A's and Queen of the Prom and married to a linebacker who's the future president of General Motors. You can imagine their surprise when they got me instead. They never have got over it. Anyway, they're not my real parents. I was found under a toadstool or something.

BEN. Are they going to be worried about you?

TRACY. Not a chance.

BEN. Then why do you want to leave?

TRACY. Why not? Look, you fish me up, we go to bed, I leave. Nice pattern there. Don't mess with patterns. Get yourself into all kinds of trouble.

BEN. You don't want to go. You were happy with me last night and you're happy right now. Why do you keep saying things you don't mean and doing things you don't want?

TRACY. Well I can't stay here forever. (*They have a staring contest which BEN wins. She surprises herself by looking away.*) Give me one good reason why I should stay.

BEN. Because you want to.

TRACY. If I want to stay then why am I leaving?

BEN. You're scared.

TRACY. Of what? You? Who the hell ARE you, anyway, Sigmund Freud? Let's just not make a big thing out of this, all right? If I want to go, I'll stay. If I want to stay, I'll go. I make my own decisions. How old are you?

BEN. Twenty-eight.

TRACY. Obviously you're too old for me. You're ancient. I'll bet you remember Howdy Doody even. And Pinky Lee. And Archduke Franz Ferdinand and Krazy Kat and Marya Ouspenskaya and Gabby Hayes and

Grover Cleveland and Mighty Mouse and don't you DARE lay a hand on me. (*BEN makes a leap at her but she eludes him, giggling. A small chase.*) Now don't you hurt me. I've very fragile, you know. (*She disappears into the kitchen, BEN close behind. From there:*) Hey. Stop it. All fingers off nipples. Hey. (*She reappears in some disarray, pulling the pyjama top back up over her shoulder and carrying an apple.*) Look what I got. I found an apple. Hey, look at this, old timer. (*BEN reappears. She is polishing the apple on her pyjamas.*) I'm going to sit right down here and eat this apple, and when I get finished I'm going to get right up and leave. (*She sits; pause.*) Well, say something. (*BEN goes and sits by his typewriter.*) Don't BROOD. I HATE brooding. (*pause*) And I don't like traps. (*She polishes. He broods.*) It's easier if you leave right away.

BEN. Easier for who?

TRACY. (*leaving the unbitten apple in her lap, not looking at him*) I'd eat you alive.

BEN. I'll take a chance. Columbus took a chance.

TRACY. I don't think you're as tough as I am. Or as smart. You'd end up miserable. You'd hate me in about three days. You'll get squashed like a bug. It isn't worth it. You gotta get some friends. You don't see any people, that's your problem.

BEN. Maybe you could help me to develop myself, be more resourceful, win friends and influence women. It'll be a learning experience.

TRACY. It'll be a whole lot of useless pain, that's what it'll be.

BEN. What's your name? You never told me.

TRACY. No, and I don't want to know yours, either. People go telling each other their names and before they know it they're somebody instead of nobody and they get trapped. I go telling you what my name is and pretty soon I'm paying half the gas bill.

BEN. My name is—

TRACY. I don't want to hear it.

BEN. My name—

TRACY. (*hands over ears*) I won't listen to this filth. Everybody ought to be anonymous.

BEN. My name is—

TRACY. ANONYMOUSANONYMOUSANONY-MOUSANONYMOUSANONYMOUSANONYM-OUS. (*Pause; she looks at him suspiciously. She takes her hands away.*)

BEN. (*quickly*) Ben.

TRACY. You bastard.

BEN. Now what's yours?

TRACY. Kiss my ass.

BEN. Is that your full name, or just what your friends call you?

TRACY. You know what I have nightmares about? There's these little tiny transparent flying things, see, I don't know what they are, but they're all sort of soft like the crap on pussywillows, you know what I mean? And they love me a lot and trust me and it'd be nice except they're so tiny and fragile I've got to watch out all the time or I'll squash them, and then there's more and more until almost all the space in the dream is filled up with them and I almost can't breathe and then somebody's calling me and I've got to go but I can't move because these damn little things are all over the place and they come right up and land on me and whisper things like music that I can't quite make out, and this person is calling me and I've got to go, so I try to get up very carefully and get away but as soon as I move I start to squash them and it's horrible but I can't stop so I keep going and every place I step I keep squashing them and they don't understand and they're screaming and they make these terrible betrayed and shocked noises and then I'm running and stumbling and squashing them everyplace and crying and there's this screaming and screaming.

BEN. And then what?

TRACY. And then I wake up and find myself having sex with some character I don't even know who is going to get in a hell of a lot of trouble if he doesn't let me get out of here quick. (*pause*)

BEN. What do you want for lunch? (*Pause; she hesitates, sighs, holds her head melodramatically, and finally gives up.*)

TRACY. Oh, well, fuck. My name's Tracy. Like in Dick Tracy.

BEN. That's a very nice name.

TRACY. (*blowing her nose loudly*) It's a stupid name. (*She takes a big bite out of the apple, then offers it to him, talking with her mouth full.*) You want a bite of this, or what?

BEN. Sure. (*He takes the apple and bites into it.*) Pretty good. (*During the following they exchange the apple, taking bites.*)

TRACY. So far. (*taking a bite*) I can leave any time, right?

BEN. That's fair. Me too, of course.

TRACY. Sure. Maybe I could stay just for a few days. Just as a humanitarian gesture on my part. But there's got to be some rules.

BEN. What kind of rules?

TRACY. Just rules. Like, don't ever expect anything from me. Just don't expect. You won't get disappointed that way. Expect nothing at all. Agreed?

BEN. What kind of rule is that?

TRACY. It's MY rule. Take it or leave it.

BEN. Any other rules I should know about?

TRACY. Just a minute, let me think about it. (*They pass the apple back and forth taking bites as she thinks.*) No telling me what to do.

BEN. No telling you what to do.

TRACY. No making fun of me.

BEN. Should I write these down?

TRACY. No cats.

BEN. No cats. No dogs?

TRACY. No dogs. No animals.

BEN. No fish? No birds?

TRACY. No fish, no birds, not any living thing.

BEN. No plants?

TRACY. Maybe plants. No, no plants. No television.

BEN. No television. No smoking?

TRACY. No smoking.

BEN. No spitting? No parking? No left turn?

TRACY. NOW CUT THAT OUT.

BEN. What have you got against cats?

TRACY. I didn't say I had anything against them. I said I don't want any around.

BEN. Why not?

TRACY. Oh, eat your apple and shut up. (*She gets up and goes towards the bedroom.*) I'm going in and get dressed.

BEN. You can't do that.

TRACY. Yes I can.

BEN. You don't have any clothes.

TRACY. Oh. I forgot.

BEN. You can wear some of mine.

TRACY. I don't like yours.

BEN. Just for this morning. Tell me what you want and what size and I'll drive into town this afternoon and get you some.

TRACY. I don't have any money.

BEN. It's all right.

TRACY. I don't want anybody buying me things.

BEN. Good. You can pay me back. Ten percent interest.

TRACY. That's robbery.

BEN. But is it against the rules?

TRACY. Okay, but only because it's an emergency. If I wear your clothes for long I'll start smelling like you. But no favors. I don't want any favors.

BEN. I'll try to keep that in mind.

TRACY. All right. (*She goes into the bedroom. Her head reappears immediately.*) And also—

BEN. What?

TRACY. Uh, well—

BEN. Speak up. I can take it.

TRACY. Also you're not a eunuch. (*She disappears into the bedroom.*)

BEN. Oh. That's nice.

TRACY. (*sticking her heud back out*) I just thought you might like to know. Big deal. (*She disappears again. From the bedroom:*) So come help me find something to put on. I think we ought to dress for lunch. Just like grown-ups.

BEN. Do they do that?

TRACY. Some do. So come help me. (*The pyjama top comes flying out the door and lands on his head.*)

BEN. I'm coming, I'm coming. (*He starts hastily into the bedroom.*)

TRACY. You forgot the apple. (*He stops, goes back for the apple, picks it up, looks back to the bedroom, thinks about it, takes a bite, goes into the bedroom.*)

ACT TWO

SCENE 3

Two months later. TRACY sits on the couch, wearing a frumpy nightgown, the tip of her cigarette glowing in the dark. After a moment BEN enters, wearing the pyjamas they shared before.

BEN. Tracy?

TRACY. Present.

BEN. What are you doing in the dark?

TRACY. Smoking a cigarette.

BEN. In the dark?

TRACY. No, in Afghanistan, what does it look like?

BEN. I thought that was against the rules.

TRACY. What rules?

BEN. Your rules.

TRACY. I forgot to tell you the most important rule, which is that I'm allowed to break all the rules.

BEN. Why are you smoking a cigarette at four o'clock in the morning?

TRACY. Four o'clock is a very good time to smoke a cigarette.

BEN. Can't you sleep?

TRACY. Could if I wanted to.

BEN. (*turning on a light*) Why don't you want to?

TRACY. I didn't say I didn't want to. I said I could if I wanted to. That doesn't mean I don't want to. Doesn't that makes sense?

BEN. I guess so.

TRACY. You don't think it makes sense.

BEN. I didn't say I didn't think—

TRACY. You didn't have to. Your voice gets patronizing, like you think I'm stupid.

BEN. I don't think you're stupid.

39

TRACY. You think everybody's dumb but you. Big man. Shakespeare. Shit.

BEN. Why don't you come back to bed?

TRACY. I don't want to.

BEN. You ought to want to.

TRACY. Why should I ought to want to?

BEN. You should ought to want to because I want you to ought to want to.

TRACY. Tough bananas.

BEN. You'll sleep through the alarm and miss your morning classes.

TRACY. No I won't.

BEN. It's the restaurant. It makes you nervous and then you can't sleep.

TRACY. What do you want me to do? Quit? You want me to quit, don't you?

BEN. It wouldn't break my heart.

TRACY. How would I pay my fees then? I'd have to drop out.

BEN. You don't have to drop out. Just find another job.

TRACY. What's wrong with the one I've got?

BEN. For one thing, you don't get home until two in the morning.

TRACY. When am I supposed to work? I go to school all day.

BEN. Also it's a seedy little dump and the proprietor is a lech and it's crawling with drug-ridden maniacs who can't keep their hands off you.

TRACY. So come down and beat them up.

BEN. I'm supposed to beat them ALL up?

TRACY. You wouldn't even beat one of them up. You never beat up anybody in your life.

BEN. I used to beat up my mother all the time.

TRACY. That's not funny.

BEN. I'm a writer, give me a break, I need my fingers to play the violin.

TRACY. You're no writer. You're a librarian.

BEN. I work in a library. That doesn't make me a librarian.

TRACY. And you write, but that doesn't make you a writer, either, right? Huh? Well?

BEN. I'll be a writer.

TRACY. If you ever finish the novel in the refrigerator.

BEN. I'll finish it.

TRACY. There's something really perverted about keeping a novel in the refrigerator, in there with the avocadoes and the lettuce and the passion fruit.

BEN. What if there's a fire or something? What if somebody should come in here and try to steal it?

TRACY. Nobody even wants to read it.

BEN. Will you please tell me what's wrong with you?

TRACY. Don't say please. I don't like it. You say please too much.

BEN. Sorry.

TRACY. And you say sorry even more too much.

BEN. What would you like me to say? Maybe I should speak in Lithuanian so you wouldn't understand me.

TRACY. Why do you want to know what I want you to say for? Why don't you just say whatever you feel like and if I don't like it I'll tell you so.

BEN. I'm sure you will.

TRACY. I don't like that.

BEN. I didn't think you would.

TRACY. You want to break up, don't you?

BEN. Break up what?

TRACY. You don't want to live with me any more.

BEN. Wait a minute. How did we get to that? Did I miss something here?

TRACY. We got to that because you won't let me

smoke and you don't like my job and you think I'm stupid and you can't stop apologizing and you beat up your mother. I guess we'll just have to break up.

BEN. I don't WANT to break up.

TRACY. Yes you do.

BEN. No I don't.

TRACY. Yes you do.

BEN. No I don't. Do you?

TRACY. Do I what?

BEN. Want to break up.

TRACY. Break up what?

BEN. (*holding his forehead in despair*) Why me, God? Why me?

TRACY. No. I thought YOU did.

BEN. Did what?

TRACY. Wanted to break up.

BEN. I don't.

TRACY. Oh. (*pause*)

BEN. Don't even think about things like that.

TRACY. I can think about anything I want to if I want to whenever I want to and you can just go suck on your typewriter.

BEN. All right, look, you can smoke cigarettes all night if you want to. Four at once. You can eat them for all I care. I just wondered why—

TRACY. I told you why.

BEN. Yes, you did, so that's all right. And I don't think you're stupid and I won't apologize any more so that's all right too, right?

TRACY. What about beating somebody up?

BEN. Why don't you just get another job?

TRACY. I don't want another job. I like it there. Those people are my friends.

BEN. You like them grabbing you all the time?

TRACY. They don't grab me all the time. You grab me all the time. Anyway, since when is it any of YOUR business? I'm not your dog. Am I your dog?

BEN. You only get like this when there's something wrong, and you never TELL me what's wrong, and by the time I figure out what exactly it is that's bothering you, it isn't bothering you any more and you deny everything.

TRACY. I must be crazy.

BEN. No, I'm crazy, I put up with it.

TRACY. I knew you wanted to break up.

BEN. Will you just stop saying that?

TRACY. Why don't you leave me alone? Why are you always bothering me?

BEN. Now you're crying.

TRACY. I'm not crying. Don't you know anything? Can't you tell when a person is crying and when she's perfectly fine? God you're stupid. Give me a Kleenex. (*He does. She blows her nose.*) Sinus.

BEN. Maybe if we just go back to bed we can talk about it in the morning. (*From TRACY, a rather hostile silence.*) Well maybe if we get some sleep we won't HAVE to talk about it in the morning. (*a decidedly hostile silence*) Okay, let's try a process of elimination. Has your mother been whining at you again about getting married? (*silence*) That's not it? Has your father started speaking to you again? No? Well, thank God for small favors. (*The silence chills further.*) That's not funny. Okay. Wasn't I very good tonight? I did my best. Would you prefer a little more violence? Whips? Funny costumes? Am I getting warmer? Can you give me a hint? Is it animal, vegetable or mineral? Two syllables? Sounds like? Didn't this used to be a conversation? Tracy? Look at me. (*No comment.*) I can see this calls for desperate measures. Don't look at me. It's better that way. I'm just going over here to the closet. (*In what follows he performs the actions he describes.*) I open the closet door. I find — AHA — ZOUNDS! — a long raincoat. From my days with Interpol. I put the raincoat on suavely over my pyjamas. 'What are you doing, Dearest?' she cannot help but ask, apprehensively. 'I'm going out,' I reply, cooly. 'Oh,' I ejaculate, 'I've forgotten my footwear. Gadzook, what footwear can I find? Hark! my galoshes! — From my days on the Pequod. — I'm putting on my galoshes now. Don't look. But, 'I SAY,' I say, 'I've forgot me headwear!' Don't look. (*He is clomping around a great deal in galoshes.*) Yikes. Begob. Just what I need, a Cleveland Indians baseball hat, autographed by John Lowenstein, a priceless chapeau. 'But where can you be going,' she implores, her voice trembling with concern. 'The night is dark and stormy, and I am afraid for you!' (*flourishing the cap high above his head*) 'Down to the restaurant,' I reply resolutely, 'to punch somebody in the nose.' (*He puts the baseball cap on his head and stomps to the door, opens it, clomps out, and slams the door.*)

TRACY. (*unable to contain herself*) YOU CAN'T GO DOWN THERE AND PUNCH SOMEBODY IN THE NOSE DRESSED LIKE AN IDIOT. (*The door opens immediately.*)

BEN. (*sticking his head back in*) SHE TALKS. (*He clomps back in.*) DO YOU SEE THAT, GOD? THIS WOMAN LOOKS RIGHT AT ME AND OPENS HER MOUTH AND TALKS. PRAISE GOD. (*He slams the door behind him.*)

TRACY. (*Having made the tactical error of looking at him, she begins to giggle in spite of herself.*) You're really dumb. You moron. You're really a moron.

BEN. (*grabbing her by the wrist and pulling her towards the bedroom*) Great. Now that we've established that you can talk and I'm a moron, let's go back to bed.

TRACY. (*getting away*) No.

BEN. Then why don't you tell me what's wrong? The suspense is killing me.

TRACY. You won't like it.

BEN. That's okay. Suffering is good for me. What is it?

TRACY. Ben —

BEN. You're pregnant.

TRACY. I'm pregnant.

BEN. I knew it. (*pause*) Is that all?

TRACY. What do you mean, IS THAT ALL? How the HELL did you know I was pregnant?

BEN. Every morning between 8:03 and 8:07 you excuse yourself politely from the breakfast table, go into the bathroom and throw up your oatmeal.

TRACY. You noticed.

BEN. I suspected.

TRACY. Why didn't you say something?

BEN. It's traditional for the woman to notice first.

TRACY. I told you you wouldn't like it.

BEN. Let me think about it a minute before you decide I don't like it.

TRACY. What's there to think about? Pregnant is pregnant.

BEN. It isn't necessarily a bad thing.

TRACY. Except that we can't afford it and aren't married and didn't want it.

BEN. Besides that it's all right.

TRACY. Besides that. Terrific.

BEN. Are we absolutely sure?

TRACY. I don't know if WE are. The DOCTOR is.

What do you think, I throw up just to keep in practice?

BEN. How long?

TRACY. How long what?

BEN. How long have you been pregnant?

TRACY. I don't know. You tell ME, Sherlock, you're so smart. What difference does that make?

BEN. It'd be nice to know when you're going to have it.

TRACY. Yeah.

BEN. Why didn't you tell me?

TRACY. I just did.

BEN. I mean, why didn't you tell me before?

TRACY. I didn't know before.

BEN. Before what?

TRACY. Before I found out. That makes sense. Doesn't that make sense?

BEN. There's no reason to get upset. The damage is already done.

TRACY. Damage. That's a nice way to put it.

BEN. I didn't mean it that way.

TRACY. What other way is there? Here's this thing growing inside me like a fungus and there goes our lives. At least MY life. I guess it doesn't do much to yours.

BEN. It does as much to me as it does to you.

TRACY. Really? You going to get up every morning and throw up with me?

BEN. Why don't you just sit down and relax?

TRACY. I AM sitting down.

BEN. Well, relax.

TRACY. I'm relaxing. Is it going to make me less pregnant? (*She gets up and begins pacing.*)

BEN. You like children.

TRACY. I hate children.

BEN. Nobody hates children.

TRACY. My father hates children.

BEN. He does not.

TRACY. He hates ME.

BEN. That's different.

TRACY. Why is it different?

BEN. I notice you're pretty jealous of other people's children.

TRACY. Whose children?

BEN. Like you wish they were yours. I've seen you.

TRACY. Your understanding of character is literary, not visceral.

BEN. What the hell does that mean?

TRACY. Visceral. It means—

BEN. I know what visceral means.

TRACY. You treat people like they were characters in books. You have no sense of cause and effect. You have no sense of reality. You have no sense. You're an idiot. They should lock you up and eat the key.

BEN. I don't understand what that's got to do with you being pregnant.

TRACY. Of course you don't. You don't understand anything about anything. And do you know why?

BEN. No. Tell me why.

TRACY. I'll tell you why.

BEN. I thought you would.

TRACY. You can't connect things up in your mind. When I tell you I'm going to meet you someplace and you go and wait there for two hours and then come home and find me sitting here eating a popsicle, what do you do? Do you yell at me? Do you beat me up? Do you throw me out? No. You come over and lick my popsicle. Like you expected me not to come but you waited anyway and then you come home and act like you're not even mad.

BEN. What flavor popsicle?

TRACY. You asshole.

BEN. So I accept you. So what?

TRACY. But you DON'T accept me. You don't even SEE me. You see some nice little drippy-eyed girl who just can't help herself because of her unfortunate childhood toilet training experiences, when in reality I am a normal healthy person who screams a lot and knows exactly what she's doing. You can't be anybody's father. You're unfit. You can't just ACCEPT your children. You've got to teach them how to handle themselves and how rotten the world is. We can't have a baby.

BEN. Well we're GOING to have one, so we'll just have to make the best of it, won't we?

TRACY. That's another thing wrong with you. You're always trying to make the best of things. Do you realize what a pain in the ass that is? There are many things you just can't make the best out of, and I'm one of them. I am not domesticable, I never WAS domesticable, and I'm never going to BE domesticable, so just forget it. Boy, I should have got out of here so fast when I could have. Babies are the worst trap there is. They make you old. We'll be OLD.

BEN. I think we ought to go to bed now and talk about it tomorrow.

TRACY. That's it, stuff it under the sheets, a little early morning fuck and a nap will make it all right. That's what got us into this damn thing in the first place.

BEN. I don't see why it SHOULDN'T be all right. I can take the novel out of the refrigerator —

TRACY. Great.

BEN. —and send it to New York—

TRACY. Send me instead, I'll go.

BEN. —and start working nights, maybe, and we can probably get some money out of your father by getting your mother to ask him so he'll give it to her and make her swear not to tell us where she got it—

TRACY. My father's a lunatic.

BEN. —and I can sell the car and we can pay one of your stupid sisters to take care of the kid while you're at school. We can do it. Hell, we can even get married.

TRACY. Who ASKED you?

BEN. So, we'll have to change a few diapers and buy a lot of stuff for it and stay home all the time and feed it in the middle of the night and I won't be able to write as much and you won't be able to study as much because of the noise and we'll be a lot poorer and your parents will be fussing around after us all the time and we won't be as free and our lives will be a little bit more ordinary and we'll be a little bit more like everybody else—(*Toward the end of this he begins to listen to himself and sounds distinctly less confident.*)—so what? (*pause*) Everybody gets old.

TRACY. Not me.

BEN. Let's go to bed.

TRACY. Our lives are ruined and all you want to do is go to bed. Why don't you hit me or something? Just once I wish you'd wind up and punch me right in the mouth. You're SO insensitive. You and me and baby shit from now on, huh? Sounds wonderful. Well if you want to sit around out here and argue with me all night, that's fine, you go right ahead. I'm going to bed. (*She stomps into the bedroom and slams the door. Pause. BEN sits there. He sighs. The door opens.*)

TRACY. (*sticking her head out*) I'm cold.

BEN. I'll be in in just a minute.

TRACY. I'm cold now. (*Pause. He doesn't move. She*

turns and goes back into the bedroom. After a moment he gets up, turns off the light, and goes into the bedroom.)

SCENE 4

The next morning. TRACY enters from the bedroom, still dressing.

TRACY. Why did you let me miss my morning classes? Do you know it's eleven thirty? What are you doing home at eleven thirty?

BEN. (*entering behind her, dressed*) I came home for lunch.

TRACY. You never come home for lunch.

BEN. Today I came home for lunch.

TRACY. Answer the question.

BEN. I forgot the question.

TRACY. Why didn't you wake me up before you went to work?

BEN. I thought you needed the rest.

TRACY. Don't you think I'm the one that ought to decide that?

BEN. You were asleep. You slept through the alarm. I tried to wake you up. You called me a dirty goat-fucker and went back to sleep. I decided you'd made your decision. I'm sorry.

TRACY. Stop saying you're sorry.

BEN. I lied. I'm not sorry.

TRACY. That's better.

BEN. Thank you.

TRACY. You're welcome.

BEN. What have we got to eat?

TRACY. A jar of mayonnaise, some maple syrup, two onions and the great American novel.

BEN. I thought you went to the store yesterday.

TRACY. I did. I got maple syrup.

BEN. Well, do you want onions and mayonnaise, or onions and maple syrup, or mayonnaise and maple syrup?

TRACY. I don't want anything. I have to go.

BEN. You don't have another class until one.

TRACY. I have to go.

BEN. Where do you have to go?

TRACY. Ben . . .

BEN. What? What's wrong? There's something wrong. You don't say Ben like that unless there's something wrong.

TRACY. Nothing's wrong. (*Pause; BEN waits.*) I know you don't really want to have a baby.

BEN. How do you know that?

TRACY. I just know.

BEN. You don't know.

TRACY. How do you know?

BEN. How do I know what?

TRACY. How do you know I don't know?

BEN. I know you don't know because I told you and I meant it when I said it and I mean it now and that's how I know you don't know whatever it was we were talking about.

TRACY. That's easy for YOU to say.

BEN. No it's not.

TRACY. You're just saying that.

BEN. If I was just saying that I wouldn't be here just saying that, I'd be on a Greyhound bus to Venezuela.

TRACY. I was talking to one of the girls at the restaurant.

BEN. I didn't know they could talk.

TRACY. She was telling me about when she got pregnant.

BEN. Sorry I missed it.

TRACY. She went to somebody.

BEN. A doctor?

TRACY. No. Well, yes, but—

BEN. A part time doctor. A veterinarian?

TRACY. LISTEN, DUMBASS.

BEN. I'm listening, I'm listening.

TRACY. She said she went to this very nice doctor and it wasn't hardly any trouble at all and then it was all over and—

BEN. Hold it, wait a minute, stop.

TRACY. It's the easiest thing in the world and—

BEN. Tracy—

TRACY. If she could do it so easy, I don't see why—

BEN. No.

TRACY. Well it isn't like it's against the law or anything.

BEN. No. End of conversation. No.

TRACY. It isn't like there's anything wrong with it, and it hardly takes any time at all, and—

BEN. I said no.

TRACY. What do you mean, NO? Just who the HELL do you think you ARE, anyway?

BEN. It's my baby, that's who I am.

TRACY. It's my baby and don't call it a baby it isn't a baby it isn't anything yet and it isn't going to be because I'm going to do it and you can't stop me.

BEN. It's as much mine as yours and you you just can't.

TRACY. Of course I can. I have an appointment this afternoon. It's all perfectly safe and legal.

BEN. You made an appointment to do that before you even told me you were pregnant?

TRACY. Don't yell at me. I wasn't going to tell you at all, but you made me last night.

BEN. You weren't even—

TRACY. What difference does it make? I should never have told you at all. Men get so hysterical.

BEN. You're incredible. All by yourself you decide to murder our child—

TRACY. Stop calling it a child. It isn't a child. It isn't anything. You can't murder somebody that doesn't exist. God, you're so stupid. Reactionary. Selfish. People do it all the time. They do it all the time.

BEN. I don't care what people do all the time. I don't do it all the time.

TRACY. I don't believe I'm having this conversation. All this time, unbeknownst to me, I've in reality been sleeping with Herbert Hoover. You didn't even know about it until last night. You've never seen it. If I hadn't told you, you'd never have known it existed. It probably looks like a fish or something now. You'll forget all about it in a couple of days and be damned happy you didn't have to spend the rest of your life worried about it.

BEN. You have no right to do that without at least—

TRACY. Some slimey little amphibian I don't even know is crawling around in my stomach and I don't have any right?

BEN. I don't care if it makes sense or not or if it seems fair or not, if you do that you can forget all about me. I won't sleep with you, I won't live in the same house with you, I won't even be able to look at you.

TRACY. What are you getting so upset about?

BEN. I don't know, but I mean it.

TRACY. Well all right, you just go right ahead. I'm pretty sick of you anyway. God, what a straight. You're just like my father.

BEN. I can't stand your father.

TRACY. You sound like the Pope or something.

BEN. If I was the Pope you wouldn't be pregnant.

TRACY. Don't bet on it.

BEN. Why are we talking about the Pope? Do I care about the Pope? WHO GIVES A GOOD GODDAMN ROYAL FLYING SHIT ABOUT THE POPE, ANYWAY?

TRACY. DON'T YOU DARE INSULT THE POPE.

BEN. I don't care what your father thinks and I don't care what's legal or how nice the doctor is or what other people think is wrong or right. This isn't happening to other people, it's happening to US, and I'm scared that if you kill that thing inside you you'll be killing us too, and I don't want that to happen.

TRACY. If you can treat me like this when I'm the one that has to be fat and sick and have the pain then maybe we're already dead. Maybe we always were. (*pause; much more quietly*) Like a potato, for instance. You don't think of a sack of old potatoes as being alive, do you? But they sit around in the cupboard and then after a while they start to sprout and there's things growing out of them and all, but it isn't like you'd say the potato was alive or anything. I mean, you wouldn't give it a name or take it to the park in a stroller or anything. It might be growing, sort of, but it isn't really alive, and it isn't really even growing, really, it's just that part of it is turning into something else. And that's all this thing inside me is doing. It's growing, sort of, but it isn't alive, it's just a part of me that got hooked up with a part of you and started turning into something else. (*pause*) It'll be like having a wart removed. That's what it's like. (*long pause*) I have to go. (*She seems to be waiting for something.*) And you'd better not try and stop me.

BEN. I don't think I'm going to try to stop you.

TRACY. You mean it's all right?

BEN. I didn't say it was all right. I said I don't think I'm going to try and stop you.

TRACY. Well, good. Because I'm going. So goodbye. (*BEN is looking at his hands. She hesitates, starts towards the door, then stops.*) Ben? Are you okay? I wish I could tell what you're thinking. You never tell me. I can't get inside you. I can't get to know you, I don't know what to do with you, it's like you're from another planet or something, you drive me nuts. (*pause*) You hate me. (*pause*) It's not yours anyway. I was pregnant when I got here. That's why I stayed. I set you up.

BEN. (*looking her in the eye*) Bullshit.

TRACY. (*looking away*) You go to hell. (*She stomps out, slamming the door behind her. BEN sits there.*)

SCENE 5

Night. Ocean sounds. BEN sits on the couch. Long pause. Then the door opens and TRACY enters quietly, looking tired. She closes the door carefully and makes a long cross to the couch, where she sits, not close to him. Pause.

BEN. Are you all right?

TRACY. Yes. I'm all right. What are you doing here?

BEN. I live here.

TRACY. I thought you were going. I thought you said you were going.

BEN. It's my house.

TRACY. Oh. That's right. I guess I should go. (*pause*) You hate me.

BEN. No.

TRACY. You HATE me.

BEN. No.

TRACY. Why not? (*pause*) You don't want me to go away?

BEN. I don't think so.

TRACY. Why not?

BEN. Why do you try to make me hate you?

TRACY. That's a lie. I never.

BEN. It isn't. You've always done it.

TRACY. That's a lie. (*pause*) No it's not. (*pause*) Why do you take it?

BEN. I asked you first. (*pause*)

TRACY. When you were little did your parents always keep giving you these animals and things, like they thought you looked like you had to have something to be grabbing onto all the time or you'd fall over or blow away or something? Well, don't look at me like that. Listen, if you don't want to hear this I can just leave, if you think this is stupid or something. I mean, you asked me a question and now I'm going to answer it, whether you like it or not. So my parents kept giving me these animals, see, not just like cats and dogs but also a pregnant racoon and two ducks named Mickey and a deflowered skunk and a chicken named Arnold and all kinds of things like that. They were really dumb. Not the animals, my parents. Well, you know how dumb they are. And the house we lived in was too close to the road, and what happens when you live too close is that all of your animals get splattered always on the road, and your brothers are always having to go out with a shovel and scrape them off and take them someplace to bury. And sometimes if they're all squashed but not quite dead your brother has to hit them with the shovel until they stop screaming or quacking or squawking or whining or meowing as the case may be. And giving them names makes it worse but I loved to and I couldn't help it and I did and when they got squashed then it wasn't just the cat or the duck it was somebody with a name that you'd lived with and slept with and talked at and listened to and fussed over and took care of and accepted you and then it was the mess that was left on the road. And after the last one was squashed which was a small bowlegged Persian kitten named Clarence aged six months who was sort of dumb and loved me a lot and never wanted any more than to just be alive and play with some piece of string or something, after that last one I made my stupid parents promise me they would never get me another thing that was alive because I had figured out what was true and still is true that there is no excuse and no way ever to make up for the millions and millions and millions of innocent betrayed and squashed up dead, and nobody's parents and nobody's God was ever going to be able to explain that to me and make it all right, and the only way not to go crazy if you had the misfortune to be a compulsive namer and lover was if you never hooked yourself up with splatterable things then it can never be your fault for needing them and having them because if you don't give you can't hurt and you don't get guilty because you can't betray if you never gave to begin with. Doesn't that make sense to you? It does make sense. It does.

BEN. Listen—

TRACY. No, I don't want to listen to you. You fouled it all up. You're so dumb. No matter what I do to you,

you just sit there and you love me. I push you away as hard as I can and you're still there. I find ten or twelve new ways to destroy you and you just keep putting yourself back together again like Humpty Dumpty. And you say you don't like being hurt or hurting back but you take everything I dish out and you don't make a big thing about it and you take care of me and you make me laugh and want to be alive and you love me and you're MUCH sicker than I am. You are out of your goddamn fucking MIND.

BEN. That was my baby, wasn't it?

TRACY. Of course it was.

BEN. Tracy—

TRACY. Just don't say anything. You still don't understand.

BEN. What don't I understand?

TRACY. I did it on purpose.

BEN. Did what on purpose?

TRACY. I sort of let it happen and it wasn't an accident exactly and it was a very stupid thing to do and don't you DARE tell me I'm crying because you're wrong and I'm not even talking in sentences any more and I don't care because I got pregnant sort of on purpose because I wanted to have a baby your baby our baby and you can just shut up and go to hell.

BEN. If you wanted to get pregnant then why did you—

TRACY. Because. I got scared. Leave me alone.

BEN. Jesus.

TRACY. You shut up about Jesus. Jesus had nothing to do with it.

BEN. All that and then—

TRACY. All that and then this.

BEN. So now you kill your own to keep the world from doing it first.

TRACY. I warned you. At the very beginning I told you how I was. I can't help it if you didn't want a baby.

BEN. I never said that.

TRACY. You didn't have to. And you never will want a baby from a worthless crazy goddamn maniac like me. You want —

BEN. Stop telling me what I want. I want YOU.

TRACY. Well, you're not going to get me. You can have your stupid house — (*She knocks over a lamp.*) — and your stupid clothes — (*She begins tearing off clothes and throwing them at him.*) — and your stupid babies. I can't live like that. I've got to get out of here.

BEN. Stop that.

TRACY. I never should have stayed here in the first place. I'm going to leave exactly the way I came. I don't want all this stuff hanging all over me. I'm going back to the ocean, that's where I'm going.

BEN. (*grabbing her*) Stop it.

TRACY. You let me go, you pig. You goddamn snake. I hate you. (*She has gotten away from him but he is now between her and the door.*) You just better get out of my way.

BEN. Nope.

TRACY. I make you miserable. I've always made you miserable. I tell lies. I don't keep promises. I make everything I touch dirty. I spoil everything. And you made me get involved when I didn't want to and now we're paying for it. Do you think I ever want to make some poor little kid put up with this all her life? She'd just grow up and be crazy and go out and find somebody else who was crazy and they'd be sick together. I've got to go back where I came from, which is nowhere, because I've been here too long and we're starting to pay. So let me go.

BEN. No.

TRACY. Anybody that really loved me wouldn't try and make me stay someplace I didn't want to be, would they? What kind of love is that when you push people around? You're just like everybody else. You just want to use me. You don't care about me. You just want to own me. And you think you can make me your own personal goddamn slave just by playing Jesus Christ all the time. What a hypocrite. What a hypocrite you are. (*BEN looks at her. He thinks about it. Then he goes over and sits down on the other side of the room. TRACY looks at the door, moves towards it, then looks back at BEN. She hesitates.*) Why can't you understand that I don't need you and I don't want you and I can't stand looking at your stupid face any more. You think I don't really mean that. You think that's just the way I have to talk to protect myself. You think underneath all this I'm really nice, but you just don't understand normal people. Normal people don't love people. Not like you want. You live in a whole different world. I've slept with more men than I can remember, even. Big, smelly, ugly men. I once slept with three men and they took turns doing it to me in the back of a truck all night and I think that was just about the best night I ever spent in my whole life. That shocks you, doesn't it? Don't try and tell me it doesn't. I can tell when somebody's shocked, and you're shocked.

BEN. What do you want, an award?

TRACY. I want to see some kind of normal human reaction out of you, that's what I want. Maybe some good old fashioned hate, for instance. I know it's in there. It's just dying to get out. Come on, Ben, you can do it. You want to bash my brains out with a crowbar, don't you? Be my guest. Let it all out, Ben.

BEN. The door's open. Nobody's stopping you. Do exactly what you please.

TRACY. You psychotic bastard. I'm a grown woman and I'm not nice and a woman doesn't have to be nice or anything else but who she is and until you can get that through your stinking stupid thick head you're just going to keep on getting sicker and sicker.

BEN. If you want to go, go.

TRACY. What do I have to do? Throw things at you? Here. (*She throws a lamp at him, just misses.*) No response. Nerves of steel. What about books? You like books. (*throwing books at him*) Try this one. How about this one? A little Shakespeare? You like Yeats? How about Freud? That's a good one. Eliot? Beckett? Faulkner? Joyce? (*She is crying, enraged, growing more and more frantic. BEN sits there.*) How about the typewriter? (*She throws the typewriter.*) Oh, wait. I know. Don't go away. (*She runs into the kitchen. Sound of refrigerator door opening and then slamming. She returns with a large manuscript.*) How about the great American novel, huh? (*She throws it at him. Pages scatter all over.*) How do you like THEM apples, Jesus? (*BEN sits there. She continues to throw things sporadically through the following.*) You thought I couldn't do that. You thought I couldn't let them drop our baby into a plastic bucket and throw it in the garbage but I did it. It was part of you and part of me and it came out slimey and they threw it away. Can't you understand that I've just murdered our child? You make me want to vomit. You're not a man. You're nothing. (*She is crying, great sobs, and stumbling around in the wreckage. Finally she bumps into the couch and falls down. She sits there in a pile of rubble on the floor, pounding a book on the edge of a table. Finally she drops the book and just sits there. Pause.*)

BEN. I think—(*hesitates*)—I think—(*hesitates*)—that—(*hesitates*)—past the words and the lies the world sits you down with two or three basic things and tells you it's time to choose. (*pause*) And I choose you. (*pause*) Your turn. (*long pause*)

TRACY. (*in a small voice*) I'm cold. I want the blanket. Could I please have the blanket? (*BEN gets up, finds the blanket, and drops it gently beside her. She pulls it around herself and sits there.*)

BEN. You must be hungry. I suppose you haven't eaten. Are you hungry?

TRACY. No. Yes.

BEN. Well. (*pause*) Anything special you'd like?

TRACY. I don't know. You try something and then I'll tell you if I like it.

BEN. All right. (*He moves to the kitchen, pauses at the door.*)

TRACY. This is never going to work. It's impossible. I'm getting out of here. I'm leaving right now. I'm going. I am. (*Pause. They look at each other. Nobody moves.*)

THE SCENE
Theresa Rebeck

Little Theatre / Drama / 2m, 2f / Interior Unit Set
A young social climber leads an actor into an extra-marital affair, from which he then creates a full-on downward spiral into alcoholism and bummery. His wife runs off with his best friend, his girlfriend leaves, and he's left with… nothing.

"Ms. Rebeck's dark-hued morality tale contains enough fresh insights into the cultural landscape to freshen what is essentially a classic boy-meets-bad-girl story."
- New York Times

"Rebeck's wickedly scathing observations about the sort of self-obsessed New Yorkers who pursue their own interests at the cost of their morality and loyalty."
- New York Post

"The Scene is utterly delightful in its comedic performances, and its slowly unraveling plot is thought-provoking and gut-wrenching."
- Show Business Weekly

OTHER TITLES AVAILABLE FROM SAMUEL FRENCH

MAKE BELIEVE
Kristin Anna Froberg

Drama / 3m., 3f.

Natasha Lisenko is twenty-two years old. She's clever, creative, can describe the plot of every episode of "Battlestar Galactica," and hasn't left the house in five years. Her sister, Lena, is an energetic, popular, occasionally cruel high-school cheerleader—or was, the last time Natasha saw her. As Natasha works her way through delayed adolescence and a strangely evolving relationship with her tutor, her family works to move forward without a sister, without a daughter, and without answers to the questions surrounding her disappearance. When the case is suddenly re-opened, Natasha is forced to make a decision. Reality or imagination? Make believe or truth? Or can she—as she's been doing for the past five years— go on existing someplace in between?

OTHER TITLES AVAILABLE FROM SAMUEL FRENCH

MEN OF TORTUGA
Jason Wells

Drama / 5m

Four men conspire to defeat a despised opponent by a ruthless act of violence: they will fire a missile into a crowded conference room on the day of an important meeting. Maxwell, a hero of the old guard, volunteers to sacrifice himself for the plan. Then Maxwell meets Fletcher, an idealist with a "Compromise Proposal" designed to resolve all conflicts. Maxwell regards the Compromise as hopeless, but he develops a liking for Fletcher - a distressing fact when Maxwell learns that, if the conspiracy proceeds, young Fletcher will be among the dead.

As the scheme spins wildly into complication, the plotters descend into suspicion, bloodlust and raucous infighting, while Fletcher is drawn, inexorably, into the lion's den.

"…Gripping…You'll be hearing more about Men of Tortuga, a blistering new play about corporate and government malfeasance from a Chicago actor named Jason Wells (who turned in the best piece of writing all year from a playwright.)…On one level, Jason Wells' elliptical drama Men of Tortuga is a genre-based thriller a la James Bond or Quentin Tarantino. But Wells is sufficiently skilled to dig deeper than that.…taut sophistication…"
- *Chicago Tribune*

CPSIA information can be obtained
at www.ICGtesting.com
Printed in the USA
BVOW08s0413290417
482536BV00009B/242/P